Crow Chief

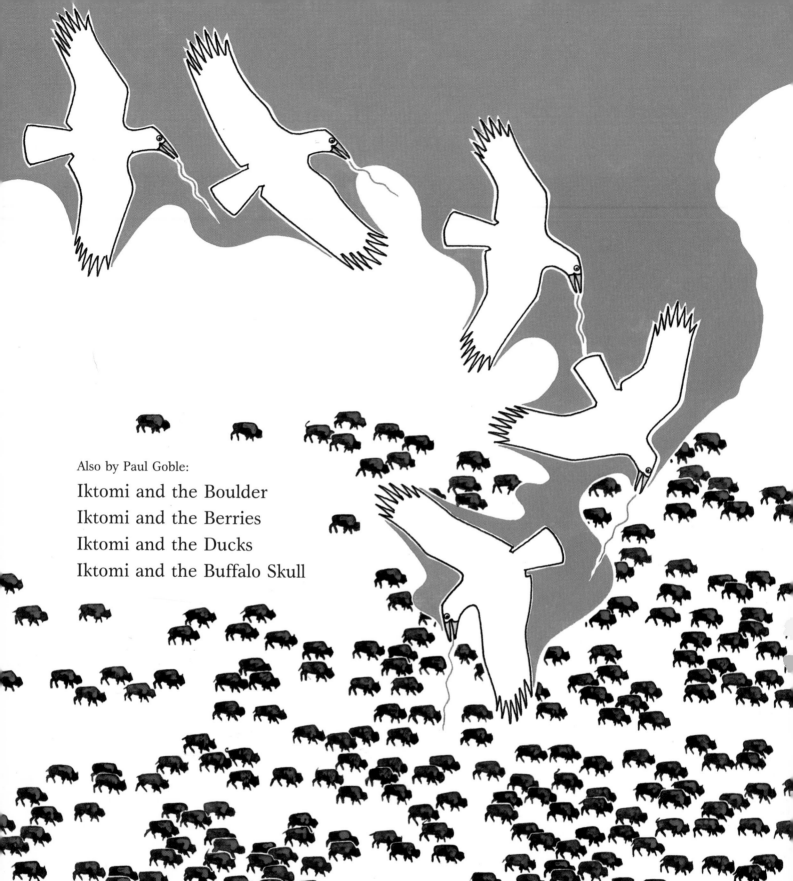

Also by Paul Goble:

Iktomi and the Boulder
Iktomi and the Berries
Iktomi and the Ducks
Iktomi and the Buffalo Skull

Crow Chief

a Plains Indian story
told and illustrated
by Paul Goble

Orchard Books, New York

for Janet and Robert, with all my love

References

Maurice Boyd, *Kiowa Voices,* Texas Christian University Press, Fort Worth, 1983. George A. Dorsey and Alfred L. Kroeber, *Traditions of the Arapaho,* Field Museum of Natural History, Anthropological Papers V, Chicago, 1903. Richard Erdoes, *The Sound of Flutes,* Pantheon Books, New York, 1976. George Bird Grinnell, *By Cheyenne Campfires,* Yale University Press, New Haven, 1926. James LaPointe, *Legends of the Lakota,* Indian Historian Press, San Francisco, 1976. John G. Neihardt, *Eagle Voice,* Andrew Melrose, London, 1953. Vivian One Feather, *Ehanni Ohunkakan,* Red Cloud Indian School, Pine Ridge, 1974. Ronald Theisz, *Buckskin Tokens,* North Plains Press, Aberdeen, 1975. Clark Wissler and D. C. Duvall, *Mythology of the Blackfoot Indians,* Anthropological Papers of the American Museum of Natural History, New York, 1909.

Copyright © 1992 by Paul Goble. All rights reserved. No part of this book may be reproduced or transmitted in any form or by any means, electronic or mechanical, including photocopying, recording or by any information storage or retrieval system, without permission in writing from the Publisher. Orchard Books, 387 Park Avenue South, New York, NY 10016. Manufactured in the United States of America. Printed by General Offset Company, Inc. Bound by Horowitz/Rae. The text of this book is set in 16 point ITC Gamma Book. The illustrations are India ink and watercolor on Oram & Robinson (England) Limited Watercolour Board, reproduced in combined line and halftone. Library of Congress Cataloging-in-Publication Data. Goble, Paul. Crow chief : a Plains Indian story / told and illustrated by Paul Goble. p. cm. Summary: Crow Chief always warns the buffalo that hunters are coming, until Falling Star, a savior, comes to camp, tricks Crow Chief, and teaches him that all must share and live like relatives together. ISBN 0-531-05947-2 ISBN 0-531-08547-3 (lib. bdg.) 1. Dakota Indians—Legends. [1. Dakota Indians—Legends. 2. Indians of North America—Great Plains—Legends.] I. Title. E99.D1G6 1992 398.2'089975—dc20 [E] 90-28457 10 9 8 7 6 5 4 3 2 1 Book design by Paul Goble

A Note about the Story

This story relates one of the many wonderful triumphs of Falling Star, the Savior. He is known to different peoples by such names as Stone Boy, Blood Clot Boy, Lodge Boy, or White Plume Boy. Henry Wadsworth Longfellow captured the spirit of similar achievements of an unspecified Iroquois or Ojibwa Savior in his familiar "Song of Hiawatha." The myths vary, but they all speak of the Savior's miraculous birth and his wisdom even as a little boy. He embodies the ideals of bravery, wisdom, kindness, and generosity. He never ages, and travels ceaselessly to help bring order to chaos, and right to wrong.

The story is far older than the coming of horses to the Great Plains, when hunting buffalo became much easier. It dates from the time when it was often difficult to kill buffalo in sufficient numbers so that everyone had enough meat during the winter months. People could not stalk the herds on the treeless plains. Instead, they killed them by a combination of skillful enticement and slow driving of herds over cliffs, through gullies, into pounds or box canyons—anywhere they could be killed easily. Many such sites are known on the plains. It was dangerous and difficult work; it could take many days, and required everyone knowing exactly what to do. Even a dog barking, a child playing, or a crow calling at the wrong moment could cause the herds to shy away, leaving people without meat, and hungry.

Much depended upon the knowledge and skill, and the sacred power, of the man who led the hunt, the "buffalo caller" as he was known. He is a powerful and truly mysterious figure in ancient Plains Indian life. Disguised as a buffalo, he would leave camp, usually for several days, patiently to draw the buffalo herds into the traps where everyone waited to kill them. He had developed a special relationship with the buffalo; he could lead them because he loved them, and understood their thoughts and fears and curiosities.

One speculates that there had to be some "explanation" for times of famine, when the buffalo caller was unsuccessful and the vast herds of buffalo would not be driven into the pounds. Perhaps the herds were simply nowhere to be found in the vicinity of the camp. At such times it must surely have seemed that even the very crows were in league with the buffalo against the hunters. Telling a story like *Crow Chief* perhaps helped both to "explain" the failure of the hunt and to turn away the terrors of famine. It was not a tale just to entertain children.

The story dates from the ancient times when Indian people hunted buffalo because that was their main food. Hunting was work. People killed only what they needed. They had no concept of today's hunting for "sport." They were in harmony with everything in nature, and had lived so for many thousands of years. They hunted as did the hawks and mountain lions, like the snakes and spiders. It was as the Creator intended. It was truly the Golden Age for Indian people.

"Caw—caw! Caw—caw!" You have heard those black crows talking to each other. Caw—caw! Caw—caw!" all day long.

Did you know that at one time crows were white?
Yes. Every member of the *Kanji Oyate*, the Crow
Nation, was white. It was long ago, long before
people had guns or horses. It was when people
hunted buffaloes with stone-headed spears and
arrows.

In those long-ago days the Crow Nation once had a great leader. They called him Crow Chief. He hated people because he wanted to be chief over everyone. But he was friends with the buffaloes. Whenever he saw hunters leaving camp, he would fly off, with his followers, and warn the buffaloes: "Caw—caw—caw! Hunters are coming! Save yourselves!"

All the buffaloes would run away. The hunters could never get near them, and so they did not bring home any meat. Nobody had enough to eat.

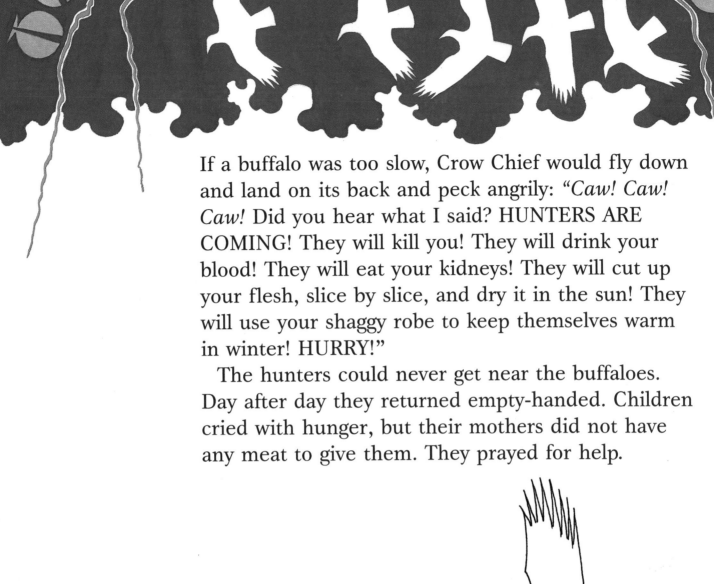

If a buffalo was too slow, Crow Chief would fly down and land on its back and peck angrily: *"Caw! Caw! Caw!* Did you hear what I said? HUNTERS ARE COMING! They will kill you! They will drink your blood! They will eat your kidneys! They will cut up your flesh, slice by slice, and dry it in the sun! They will use your shaggy robe to keep themselves warm in winter! HURRY!"

The hunters could never get near the buffaloes. Day after day they returned empty-handed. Children cried with hunger, but their mothers did not have any meat to give them. They prayed for help.

Their prayers were answered: a young man called
Falling Star came to the camp. He is always traveling
from one place to another to rescue people who are
in trouble. He listened to their story, and promised
to help.

  "Bring me a buffalo robe which has the horns and
hoofs attached to it," Falling Star told the people.
"Pitch a tipi at the center of the camp circle, and
paint buffaloes on the outside. Tomorrow morning,
let the hunters go out, just as usual."

When the sun was setting, Falling Star told the people: "Go to your tipis now. Put out your fires, close the smoke flaps, tie down your doors, and keep silence. Mothers, do not even let your babies cry."

Falling Star chose a young man to go with him, and they shut themselves inside the painted tipi. Soon there were faint sounds of singing, the beat of a drum, rattles shaking. They were talking to the buffalo spirits.

Early the next morning Falling Star and the young
man walked out of the tipi. They were hidden
underneath the robe, pretending to be a buffalo bull.

Crow Chief was still half-asleep. He thought it was
just an aged bull who had wandered off during the
night and was plodding back to join the herd.

Crow Chief watched the hunters sharpening their knives and stringing their bows. When they left camp, he flew off, as he always did, to warn the buffaloes: "*Caw—caw!* Hunters are coming!"

The herd started to run, and soon the sound of their hoofs was like thunder as they stampeded away.

Not the old bull....He fell further and further behind. "Are you deaf, you decrepit old bull?" Crow Chief screamed. "RUN! If the hunters don't get you, the wolves soon will. *Caw—caw!* HURRY!"

Crow Chief flew down and pecked angrily at the old bull's back. At that very instant Falling Star reached up and caught Crow Chief by his legs! Yes! That wicked bird was a prisoner! At last!

They tied his legs together and carried him home, upside down, squawking and swearing and furiously flapping his wings.

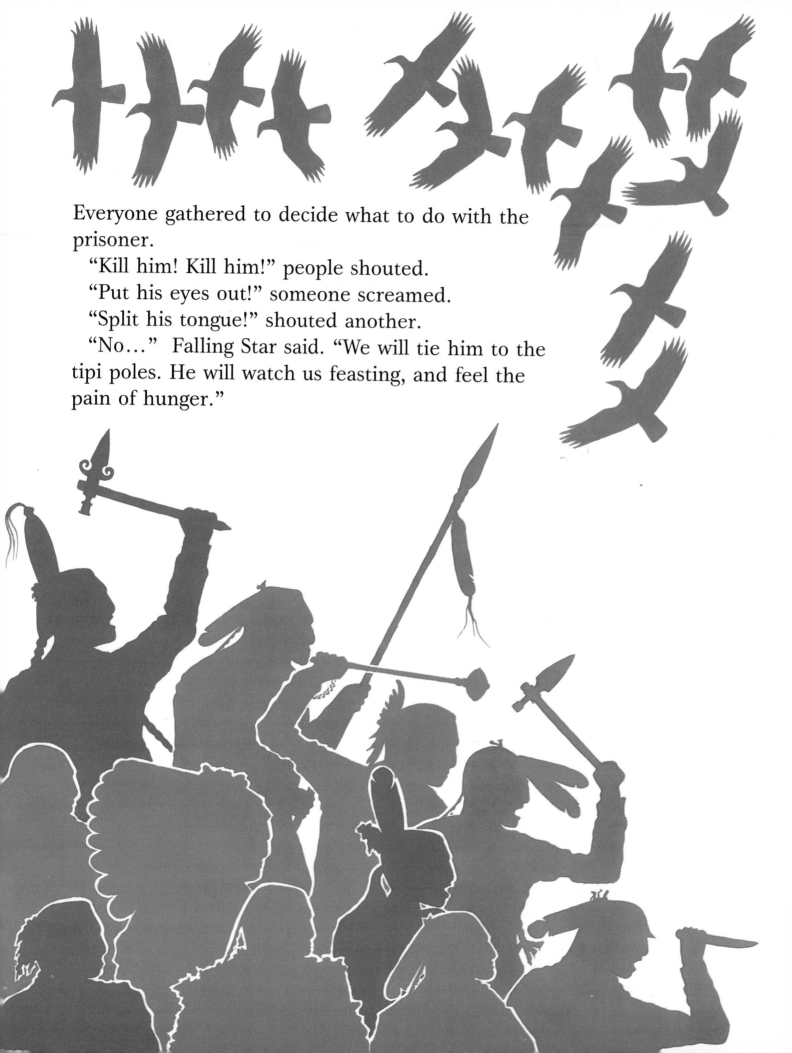

Everyone gathered to decide what to do with the prisoner.

"Kill him! Kill him!" people shouted.

"Put his eyes out!" someone screamed.

"Split his tongue!" shouted another.

"No…" Falling Star said. "We will tie him to the tipi poles. He will watch us feasting, and feel the pain of hunger."

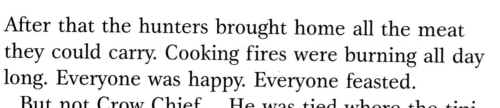

After that the hunters brought home all the meat they could carry. Cooking fires were burning all day long. Everyone was happy. Everyone feasted.

But not Crow Chief....He was tied where the tipi poles cross together. He had to sit in the smoke and the delicious aroma of the cooking fire down below. They kept him a prisoner until his feathers were black with soot.

"Have pity on me! *Onshimala ye!* Have pity on me!" he cried again and again.

One day Falling Star untied his legs and said: "The Creator told us to share and live like relatives together. Do not forget again. From now on your people will always be black feathered, as a reminder. Go!"

Crows have been black ever since. They never forget. They are still talking about it. Every mother crow tells the story to her young ones. It is true.

After that they followed behind the hunters to eat the pieces of meat which the hunters left for them. Everyone got enough to eat. There was peace.

Falling Star still travels from one place to another to help people. One day, when we need him, he will come again.

"*Caw—caw! Caw—caw!*" You have heard those black crows talking to each other. "*Caw—caw! Caw—caw!*" all day long.

Old Songs about the Crow:

From all over the earth they are coming:
A Nation is coming!
A Nation is coming!
The Eagle has brought the news to the People.

From over the whole earth they are coming:
The Buffaloes are coming!
The Buffaloes are coming!
The Crow has brought the news to the People.
        (Lakota)

The Crow circles above me.
The Crow circles above me.
He has come to take me up.
        (Arapaho)

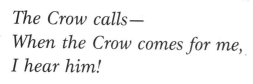

I can hear everything—
I am the Crow.
        (Arapaho)

The Crow calls—
When the Crow comes for me,
I hear him!
        (Arapaho)